For Natalia

pork +

In this story ...

SUGAR - Hannah's toy fairy. Her skin changes colour, her magic dust can make you grow (or shrink) and she sings ALL THE TIME!

BLAZE - My toy dragon. He snorts fire and he can fly but he is a bit scared of pretty much everything.

HANNAH - I've tried to draw her name to show you what she's like. She jumps into things and has lots of feelings and stuff.

JO - That's me! I'm just me really. But every time we have a magical adventure with Sugar and Blaze, I'm the one who writes it down.

THIS is our latest adventure...

The Sugar and Blaze Adventures
Have you read them all?

That's Rubbish! ☐

Tinselpants! ☐

TINSELPANTS!

Jenny York

ILLUSTRATED BY LUKE, JOSIE and HANNAH COLLINS

For all the
Harmers, Nowaks and Parkins
(the most tree-mendous friends)
Merry Christmas!
with love x

Find out more about
Jeny York by
visiting
www.jennyyork.com

First published in Great Britain in 2020 by Saltaire Books, Bradford,
England.

CHAPTER ONE

It was Christmas time!

Now in my opinion, Christmas is the very best time of year.

Especially if it snows!

But even if it doesn't snow, Christmas means presents and decorations and **fun stuff**. Like the School Christmas Fair.

That's where this story starts actually, with the Christmas Fair.

Because if we **hadn't won the raffle, it might have been a perfectly normal**

Christmas...

Dad, Hannah and I had just got back from the Christmas Fair, our hands full of sweets and treats and sparkly bags.

"How was it?" asked Mum, raising an eyebrow.

"It was brilliant!" said Hannah. "And look what we won!"

Mum ducked back slightly as Hannah waved a toy in her face.

(My little sister can get a bit over-excited sometimes and it's best to protect your eyes when she does.)

"It's an Elf-on-the-shelf!" squealed Hannah.

Mum shot Dad one of her 'looks'.

"I thought we agreed not to buy one of those," she said.

"We didn't **buy** it," Dad grinned. "We **won** it! And that's completely different."

"Yep!" agreed Hannah, beaming. "Dad

bought <u>thousands</u> of tickets, nearly all of them actually, and then..."

"Woah, woah, woah!" said Dad quickly, glancing at Mum. "**How** we won it isn't important Hannah. The point is, Mum said not to buy one and we didn't buy one."

Mum rolled her eyes.

"We already have something that causes a **magical amount of mess**," she grumbled. "In fact, it's more like three 'somethings'... You lot!"

Dad ignored that and grabbed the Elf. He made its arms reach out towards Mum as if it wanted a hug.

"C'mon!" said Dad in a squeaky Elf voice, "Give me a chance. **I'm Christmassy!**" Mum snorted a laugh. "Fine!" she sighed. "I give up. I just don't see how making a mess is Christmassy."

"Well never mind that right now," said Dad. "We have more important things to think about. Did you get the tree?"

Mum smiled and nodded.

"And it's a really good one!" she shouted after us as we **SPRINTED** to the sitting room to check it out.

Mum was right! It was BRILLIANT!

This year's Christmas tree was loads taller than last year and twice as bushy. A Christmassy pine-tree smell was already filling the room.

"It's perfect!" breathed Hannah, next to me and I nodded.

As I turned round to look for the decorations box, Dad waddled into the room. He was completely covered in tinsel with a bauble in each hand and a star stuck in his hair!

"We don't need that stinky old twig," he announced, **"I'm being the Christmas tree this year!"**

Hannah burst out laughing.

"Dad, you can't be a Christmas tree," I grinned.

"Why not?" he frowned. "People are always saying, *'You can be whatever you want to be!'* **Well I want to be a Christmas tree."**

"Since when?" asked Mum, staggering in with a gigantic box of decorations.

"It's quite a new dream," admitted Dad.

Mum laughed and began rummaging in the

box.

"Hold on, hold on!" cried Dad, shrugging himself out of his tinsel. **"I've had another idea."**

He picked up some tinsel and started rolling it into balls and stuffing it into the branches. Then he grabbed a red strand from the box and draped it in a long U shape.

"There we are! Finished!" he smiled, pointing at the tree.

He had given the tree a smiley face!

"Unless you think it should be winking?" he added uncertainly.

Mum looked at Hannah. Hannah looked at me...and then all three of us exploded into fits of giggles.

"What?" asked Dad, pretending to be offended. **"It's perfect. No one wants a sad Christmas tree!"**

"I think we should use at least some of the decorations," suggested Hannah hopefully.

"Alright, alright..." said Dad. **"...You can add a few more bits if you must. But don't knock off the face. It's an important part of the overall design!"**

"OK Mr Christmas Tree," said Mum, smiling and pulling the star out of Dad's hair. "Let's make something MAGICAL."

We all nodded... but at that point we had no idea just how magical it would turn out to be!

CHAPTER TWO

Now at this point in the story, you might be thinking the naughty elf is somehow sending Dad bonkers. But actually my Dad is that silly **all the time.**   (You'd be right to keep an eye on the elf though!)

Anyway, I don't know what your tree is like, but our tree is like **chaos on a stick!**

Because you see, my Mum likes to keep **EVERYTHING!** And I mean **everything.** So along with the usual million baubles and miles of tinsel, there's...

a knitted Christmas pudding
(from Granny - she knits a lot),

a glittery golden
triceratops,

and a load of random nonsense Hannah and I
made at school:

No idea what this is.

Made by me in nursery.

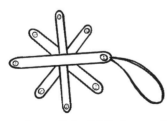

At least 6 years old.
<u>Do not eat</u>.

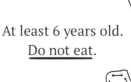

Snowflake? Ninja star?

It doesn't matter how old, broken or insane a decoration is, everything goes on the tree.

"Aha!" cried Dad rummaging through the decorations box. **"Here he is! General Red!"**

He pulled out a battered old toilet roll, painted to look like a robin.

"I made this little guy **when I was at school**," he said proudly, thrusting it into the branches. "Best to put him up high **so he can keep an eye on things."**

Dad winked.

"Just the one eye," he added with a grin.

General Red (the robin toilet roll) had lost one of his eyes many Christmases ago. Luckily Dad had fixed the situation by drawing on a pirate's eye patch.

"Oh, look," said Mum, lifting a sleigh decoration out of a tiny padded box. **"This is 80 years old, you know!** It was bought for your Grandad, for his very first Christmas."

This decoration didn't go on the tree any more. It had its own special place on the shelf, where it was extra safe. Mum popped it there now and sighed.

"This tree is missing something!" said Dad, tapping his chin thoughtfully. **"Aha!"**

He **DASHED** from the room but was back **IN A FLASH**.

"Crackers!" said Dad proudly, holding a packet of cheesy biscuits. "For the tree!"

"You're crackers!" teased Mum, shaking her head.

"What?" said Dad. "The internet says lots of people put crackers on their tree."

"It means the snappy, banging things," laughed Mum. **"You can't put cheesy biscuits on a Christmas tree."**

"Don't see why not," sulked Dad. "It's no crazier than the rest of the things on it."

He did have a point!

"Sometimes people hang candy canes on Christmas trees," suggested Hannah.

Dad nodded enthusiastically and **WHIZZED** off to the kitchen once more.

When he came back this time, he was clutching a packet of chocolate chip cookies!

"This is all we have," he shrugged, trying without much luck to balance them on the branches. "**Unless we go with leftover sausages?** I did see some of those in the fridge...?"

"Absolutely not!" said Mum. "No sausages!"

"I was thinking we could lash them together to make a sort of meaty tinsel," said Dad, wiggling his eyebrows.

I had a sudden image of a meaty Christmas tree.

It would have...

a chicken star

meatball baubles

strings of sausage tinsel

I was just imagining Dad dipping beef burgers in glitter when Hannah had a fabulous idea...

CHAPTER THREE

"Did you know the Harmer kids camp out under their tree in sleeping bags!" she said. "Just on the night they finish decorating it. Could we do that?"

Mum looked thoughtful.

"Would you be OK, downstairs on your own?" she asked.

"We'd be fine," grinned Hannah. "Sugar and Blaze would be with us!"

Sugar was Hannah's toy fairy and Blaze was my toy dragon.

No one else knew, but Blaze and Sugar were not your average toys.

They came to life!

Mum kept hinting that I was too old for a bedtime toy, but I ignored her.

Blaze was a fire breathing dragon. He could fly! AND, with the help of Sugar's magical fairy dust, he could grow big enough to carry us... LIKE A PLANE!

That's the kind of toy I planned on keeping around!

Because ever since we got Sugar and Blaze, some odd things have been happening to us... weird, magical stuff!

Mum smiled.

"I suppose camping out under the Christmas tree **does** sound like a fun Christmas tradition," she agreed before muttering, **"better than that elf nonsense anyway!"**

****

So later that night, we snuggled down in our sleeping bags under the Christmas tree. The fairy lights gave the room a cosy glow and General Red watched over us with his single beady eye.

Mum had taken Dad's cookies back out of the tree but there was always a chance she'd missed one or two. Maybe we could have a midnight feast! This was going to be great!

Mum and Dad said 'good-night' and the moment they went upstairs…

…the toys came to life!

Oh Christmas tree
how love-love-love
leeeeeee are your
branches - be-do-do
do-branches
YEAH!

sang a shrill voice.

"Hi, Sugar!" whispered Hannah.

"Can't you be quiet for one second!" grumbled Blaze. "Mum and Dad will come back down if you keep making all that racket!"

Sugar shot her noise cancelling magic at the doorway.

"Happy now-ow-ow?" she sang gleefully.

Sugar loves singing. She sings all the time.

It drives Blaze totally bonkers!

Another thing you should know about Sugar

is that when she comes to life she changes colour **a lot**, depending on her feelings.

In the sparkle of the Christmas tree lights her skin was a bright golden yellow. (That was her joyful colour.)

She's always happy when she's annoying Blaze.

"What a tree-mendous tree," whispered Blaze, smiling shyly at his joke. "Oh, Christmas is so exciting! What have you been up to? **Tell us everything!**"

Blaze **loves** to hear about the exciting things we do each day. He's very easily impressed because he's the sort of dragon that has to work quite hard to be brave sometimes.

"I won an Elf," Hannah whispered. "I'm going to call him Elfie! I'm not sure where I put him, but I can show you tomorrow."

"**An elf! Reeeeeeeeally!**" sang Sugar. "**A BOY ELF**? **How looooooooooooooovely!**"

"Sugar!" said Blaze, sternly. "Not this again!"

"Whaaaaaat?" she asked innocently. **"I'm just being interested."**

Blaze rolled his eyes.

"Although. . ." Sugar grinned. **"Maybe we WILL fall in love. . ."**

Blaze pretended to be sick.

"And then I could sing 'All I want for Christmas is yoooooooooooo' at him."

"I think you mean **to** him," said Blaze.

"**Whatever!**" Sugar shrugged. "**All I waaaaaaant...**"

"Please, let's just change the subject," Blaze begged, covering his ears.

So we told them all about Dad wanting to put food on the tree and about General Red, and Grandad's special sleigh decoration.

After a while, Hannah's voice drifted off and I heard her snuffly snores. And then, Sugar's little snore-y squeaks.

"Time to go to sleep," I told Blaze, but he didn't answer.

He must havc already nodded off.

I wriggled down deeper into my sleeping bag and fell asleep.

Until just before midnight...

CHAPTER FOUR

It was the Christmas tree that woke me up!

Don't worry. It wasn't the smiley face starting to talk or anything like that. No, it was actually the lights.

The lights on the Christmas tree had changed to disco-mode, flashing in crazy blasts of colour.

And then I noticed the really weird thing. Except for the lights, the tree was completely EMPTY!

Next to me Hannah sat up, her face changing

colour in the dancing lights.

"What's happening?" she mumbled sleepily.

"This is bad!" squeaked Blaze. "Really bad!"

He flew up to perch on my shoulder and I felt him give a little spooked-out shudder.

"Sugar, wake up!" hissed Hannah.

"Whas-wasa-matter?"asked Sugar, trying to cover her eyes as Hannah turned her towards the disco tree.

"Look!" Hannah insisted. "Someone has stolen all our decorations!"

Sugar squinted at the tree trying to focus... she rubbed her eyes... and then...

"Ahhh. Fab-uuuu-lous!" she cried. "A tree party! I love a good tree party!"

I felt Blaze relax on my shoulder.

"Oh... yeah, of course," he said. "I knew that. I knew it was just a tree party. I wasn't scared."

"What on earth...?" grumbled Hannah. "What's a tree party?"

Sugar flew to the tree and gestured around the branches dramatically.

"The night after a Christmas tree is decorated, all the decorations come to life..." sang Sugar. **"...for a party! Now that's my kind of magic!"**

"I'm not seeing a party," said Hannah, frowning and looking round. "Where exactly...?"

"The Christmas magic opens a door to a hidden room, deep inside the treeeeeee," explained Sugar.

"That can't be right," I said. "If this was really happening on EVERY tree, EVERY year someone would have seen it happen by now!"

"The Christmas magic hides it," said Sugar simply. **"If your Mum and Dad were here right now, they'd see every decoration in its place."**

"Then why can we see the empty tree?" I demanded.

"Probably for the same reason you see everything magical these days..." shrugged Sugar.

"...Because you're with us!" finished Blaze.

At that moment, there was a rustling noise and the tree started to shake and shudder until...

...a jolly, white...

snowman

fell out of the branches with a

BUMP!

Meeeeeeerry Christmas! he cried, flinging his arms wide. **"Here for the party,**

are you? It's mad! An absolute whopper! Meeeeeeeeerry Christmas!"

He gave his fat bottom a jolly shake and started to climb back into the tree.

"Wait!" I gasped. "You're the snowman I made in Nursery!"

He turned back to look at me with a grin.

"Am I?" he giggled. "Well, you did a great job! Meeeeeeeeeerry Christmas!"

And again he jiggled his bum.

"This – is – amazing!" said Hannah, "Decorations coming to life! Wait a minute! What about those posh trees that only have baubles? Do they still get a party?"

"Are you kidding?" asked Sugar. "Posh bauble parties are WILD!"

"That's right," agreed Blaze. "They mostly just roll around telling jokes and giggling.

"I actually know their favourite

joke," added the snowman helpfully. "**Would you like to hear it? Meeeeeeeeeeeeerry Christmas!**"

Hannah nodded.

"**Oh, I do like that one!**" giggled the snowman, wiping tears from his eyes. "**Merry Christmas!**"

And still chortling to himself, he gave his bum another joyful wiggle.

"You say 'Meeeeeeeerry Christmas' a

lot!" smiled Hannah.

"Well, I think I'm supposed to say it a lot," beamed the snowman, "because you see, it's written on my bum. LOOK!"

And before we could object, he bent over and wiggled his bum in our direction.

Sure enough in my scrawled, baby handwriting, there it was. Like the world's most Christmassy bum tattoo.

"Meeeeeeerry Christmas!" added the snowman, as if to prove his point.

Well, what do you say to that?

"Erm..." I tried, "...sorry about writing on your, erm... you know."

And I gestured vaguely towards his bum as he stood up.

"Don't worry about it!" he shrugged. "It says Jo somewhere, too but that's not my name."

"No," I said, feeling more and more embarrassed by the second, "that's actually **my** name."

"REALLY?" he cried. "What a coincidence. Wait! Does that mean my name's written on your bum?"

Sugar and Hannah erupted into fits of giggles at this.

"Because if you wanted to check," he added, "my name is Tinselpants! Meeeeeeeerry Christmas!"

I not gonna lie. I was definitely blushing by

this point.

"**Tinsel pants!**?!" squeaked Sugar, through gasps of laughter. "**PANTS? Oh, stop it! This is too good to be true!**"

"I know, right?" giggled the snowman, starting to bounce in circles. "Isn't it a fabulously silly name! Tinselpants!"

Sugar linked hands with him to make a bouncing circle while Hannah clapped and they all chanted.

Tinselpants, Tinselpants,

Tinsel–Tinsel–Tinsel–pants!

"Now, really..." began Blaze, disapprovingly. But, at that moment,

something dark

swept over

our heads!

CHAPTER FIVE

"WHAT'S GOING ON DOWN HERE?" barked a rough voice.

It was Dad's robin decoration, swooping and soaring around our heads like a real-life bird!

He landed on the bottom of my sleeping bag, coming to a stop with three springy hops.

Tinselpants stood to attention, looking guilty.

"Nothing's going on, General Red, Sir," lied Tinselpants. "I was just very quietly chatting to these children. Whispering, in fact! We were whispering.

The one-eyed robin peered at us and gave a few more angry hops.

"WELL THAT IS STRICTLY AGAINST THE RULES," he snapped. **"THE RULES CLEARLY STATE THAT NO DECORATION MAY LEAVE THE TREE."**

Blaze bit his bottom lip, looking worried. He hates breaking rules. But Tinselpants just grinned.

"Then what are you doing out here, General?" he asked sweetly.

The robin puffed out his red chest in outrage.

"I'M ON A SPECIAL MISSION," he said sternly, **"GLITZEN, THE GOLDEN TRICERATOPS, HAS DISAPPEARED!"**

"Well, it is a party," said Sugar, shrugging. "He's probably just wandered off."

"WANDERED OFF!" he cried, turning on Sugar. **"AWAY FROM THE TREE! NEVER!"**

His eyes darted around the gloomy corners of the room, searching.

"SOMETHING'S NOT RIGHT!" he sniffed. **"I FOR ONE AM KEEPING AN EYE ON THAT ELF!"**

Hannah frowned while General Red continued to grumble to himself.

"IN MY DAY CHRISTMAS WAS ABOUT REAL TRADITIONS LIKE EATING TOO MUCH AND WATCHING TV!"

"Hold on," interrupted Hannah. "Are you talking about my Elf on the Shelf?"

"OH IT'S YOURS, IS IT?" scowled General Red.

"Well, yes," admitted Hannah, hesitantly. "I won him at the Christmas Fair. But he's just a toy."

"TOY, INDEED!" spat General Red. **"I'VE READ THE INTELLIGENCE REPORTS ON THOSE THINGS. NOTHING BUT TROUBLE."**

"Really?" squeaked Blaze, glancing around.

General Red nodded.

"OH YES! STARTS WITH A BIT OF SILLINESS. MAYBE A DECORATION GOES MISSING..." he gave Sugar a pointed look. **"AND BEFORE YOU KNOW IT, THE CAT'S DISAPPEARED!"**

"But, Mr. General Red, Sir," tried Hannah, soothingly. "We don't have a cat!"

The robin twitched his head in alarm.

"WHAT?!? CAT'S GONE MISSING TOO?!" he spluttered. **"WELL, I TRIED TO WARN YOU."**

I had a sudden image of Hannah's Elf carrying a full sized cat on it's back and tried not to laugh.

"General Red, listen!" cried Hannah. "There's no missing cat."

But General Red wasn't listening at all. He was hopping backwards and forwards looking absolutely frantic.

Hop, hop, hop! Hop, hop, hop!

"Oh, look how he bobs along!" sang

Sugar. **"Like in that song**. . .

When the
red, red, oooh so red
robin goes
bob, bob, bobbidy
bobbing
alooooooong!

Sugar pointed but General Red was suddenly perfectly still...and glaring.

"MADAM," he said coldly, **"I DO NOT BOB, BOB, BOB!"**

But on the last 'bob' he did another little bob by accident - which was pretty funny!

Luckily, before Sugar could laugh (or even worse, start singing again) Tinselpants bounced forward.

"Time to get back to the party!" he said. "I can show you around, if you like? Be your guide? Merry Christmas!"

"**Sounds wonderful!**" sang Sugar, flying over and pulling Hannah to her feet.

"WOAH, WOAH, WOAH! HOLD YOUR REINDEERS THERE!" said General Red, flying in front of them.

"ARTICLE 2.1 OF THE TREE PARTY TREE-TY STRICTLY FORBIDS NON-MAGICAL BEINGS FROM ENTERING."

Sugar gasped.

"**How dare you!**" she sang. "**I am a fairyyyyyyy!**"

General Red didn't budge.

"AND WHAT ABOUT HER?" he barked, pointing to Hannah.

"**Oh, she's a fairy too**," lied Sugar breezily. "**She's with me.**"

General Red turned to Hannah who had hastily crossed her fingers behind her back and was nodding furiously.

"WITH ALL DUE RESPECT MISS, YOU ARE NOT A FAIRY AND YOU MUST GO BACK TO SLEEP!"

Sugar stamped her foot.

"This iiiiiis an outrage," she sang. **"I'm going to stand her and siiiiiing until you see seeeense. . . Christmaaaaaaaas! Chriiiiii-iiiii-iist- maaaa- ah -ah -as!"**

"ARGH!" yelled the robin, trying to hide his head under his wing! **"ARGH. MAKE IT STOP!"**

"It's OK, Sugar!" said Hannah quickly. "You and Blaze go without us. We probably should be getting back to sleep."

Sugar looked between Hannah and the tree, clearly undecided. But in the end her love of a party won.

"Well, if you're sure?" she sang looking a bit guilty.

"Absolutely sure," said Hannah, "General Red can keep an eye on us, can't you

General?"

"MISSION ACCEPTED," he cried twisting his wing into a salute.

So Sugar and Blaze flew into the tree with Tinselpants clambering after them and under the single beady eye of General Red, we settled down to sleep.

But almost immediately the tree rustled again!

"WHO'S THERE?" demanded the General. **"SHOW YOURSELF!"**

No-one did! Instead, a pine cone

WHIZZED out and **clonked** General Red on the head!

"THOSE BAUBLES!"

he spluttered in outrage.

"THEY'VE GONE TOO FAR THIS TIME! I'LL TEACH THEM TO..."

He darted off into the tree...and as he did so a squeaky giggle echoed around the darkness.

CHAPTER SIX

"OH, I DO LOVE MAKING MESS!" giggled the squeaky voice.

But it wasn't a bauble... It was Elfie!

"Look!" said Hannah.

There, up in the tree, was Hannah's toy from the fair! Except, he wasn't a toy anymore...

He was very much alive!

And he had Sugar!

She was bright red with anger and struggling furiously, but it looked like she couldn't break free.

"LET'S SMASH STUFF!" cried Elfie snatching up Mum's special glass snowflake! **"THAT ALWAYS MAKES A MESS!"**

The others were coming out of the tree now. Blaze and Tinselpants and the General. They were all watching the elf warily. Like he was a bomb that could go off any second.

"L-l-let her go," stammered Blaze, "and no one needs to get hurt!"

"I'M ALREADY HURT!" screeched the elf, a

mad look in his eye. **"NO INVITE TO YOUR STUPID PARTY! NO PLACE ON YOUR STUPID TREE!"**

And with that, he threw the glass snowflake at the floor.

With lightening reflexes, Blaze swooped through the air and caught it.

Elfie snarled.

Hannah scrambled towards the tree. She reached out to grab Elfie but he disappeared with a

PING

and reappeared on the bookcase holding a pottery angel.

"LET- ME- GO!" panted Sugar, wriggling furiously.

"NO!" giggled Elfie, and he threw the pottery angel at the floor.

Again, Blaze swooped and snatched it out of the air, but it was only a matter of time before something smashed!

All I can say is thank goodness for Sugar's noise cancelling magic. Mum and Dad would have been having a crazy night without it!

"ENOUGH," shouted General Red. **"ELF - YOU PUT THAT FAIRY DOWN, RIGHT NOW!"**

Elfie just laughed.

"NOT A CHANCE, YOU UGLY, OLD SPARROW!" he giggled. "YOU SEE, I NEED HER MAGICAL DUST."

PING

Elfie disappeared and re-appeared, balancing on a shelf. He grabbed Grandad's sleigh decoration.

PING

The next second, he was back on the floor

snatching something golden from behind the curtains.

The missing triceratops!

With another magical...

PING

...he unlocked the patio doors and sprang outside with the decorations, shaking Sugar as he ran.

"Stop it!" shrieked Sugar, pounding Elfie with her tiny fists. **"This** (shake, shake) **is an absolute** (shake, shake) **outrage!"**

But clouds of Sugar's sparkling dust now billowed out all around them. And inside the clouds the dust was working its magic.

The decorations grew and grew until Elfie was as tall as Hannah! Worse than that, he now had a massive sleigh and a pony-sized dinosaur to pull it!

He tossed Sugar back into the house and leapt into the sleigh.

"STOP!" screamed Hannah. "That's Grandad's sleigh! You give it back!"

She snatched up Mum's nutcracker ornament as a weapon and charged outside!

We all ran after her, but just as she got to the sleigh...

A golden force field expanded around the sleigh, throwing Hannah backwards.

"DON'T YOU JUST LOVE CHRISTMAS MAGIC?" Elfie giggled. "YOU CAN'T COME NEAR ME! HA-HA!"

And with a jingle, he shook the reins of the triceratops and the sleigh whisked him away into the starry night.

"No! NO! NO!" cried Hannah, getting back to her feet.

I turned to Sugar and Blaze.

"We have to get that sleigh back!" I said.

"And stop the elf," agreed Blaze, nodding. "Or who knows what he'll do!"

"And we need to bop him on the head with a nutcracker!" sang Sugar grimly. "I want reveeeeeeeeenge!"

"Well, we can't just chase him. Not now he has that sleigh," pointed out Tinselpants. "Meeeerry Christmas!"

"GOOD POINT," nodded General Red. **"EXACTLY HOW OLD IS THAT DECORATION, CHILDREN?"**

"About 80 years," I said. "Why? What does it matter?"

"Decorations soak up the magic of Christmas," explained Tinselpants. **"Meeeer..."**

"Meaning?" snapped Hannah impatiently.

"Meaning that sleigh has built up 80 years of power," said Tinselpants. **"and it'll protect the Elf with everything it's got. Meeeeeerr...."**

"But why?" I asked.

Tinselpants looked sad.

"Because it thinks it's protecting it's normal rider...Santa!" he explained.

"And also, Merry Christmas," he muttered under his breath.

"So it's impossible!" cried Hannah.

"NOT IMPOSSIBLE," said General Red, shaking his head. **"BUT YOU WILL NEED A POWERFUL MAGICAL OBJECT TO DEFEAT HIM!"**

"And where do we get one of those, exactly?" I asked.

"You'll need to go right to the top!" grinned Tinselpants. "The top of the earth that is!"

"You don't mean. . .?" sang Sugar.

"The North Pole!" cried Tinselpants, and his snow seemed to sparkle at the thought of it. "If you want to stop that elf, you'll need a magical gift...from Santa!"

CHAPTER SEVEN

Now, I think I mentioned back in Chapter 3 that if you sprinkle Blaze with Sugar's magical dust he can grow to the size of a small plane.

So anyway, that's what we did!

We magic-blasted Blaze to full size and set off on his back, soaring over the sea towards the North Pole... and Santa!

Hannah and Sugar belted out rowdy Christmas songs into the chilly night air and I clutched Tinselpants so he didn't blow away.

Because our new snowman friend had insisted on coming along to be our guide. The only problem was, **he was a Christmas tree decoration!** He'd never left the tree before, let alone the house. So his tour had gone a bit like this:

Ooh! Blue Swimming ice badgers! They're almost extinct!

and then...

Wow! Sea Squirrels burying their nuts in the waves!

and then...

They look like big waves, but really they're Nard Walloons.

We had just passed a very alarmed seagull that definitely wasn't a "trump-wuzzle" when Sugar stopped singing and gave a deep sigh.

"Time for a break Blaze," she called. **"I know a great place. Take a left and keep your eyes peeled."**

"But what are we looking for?" I asked, frowning. "There's nothing out here in the middle of nowhere."

"Wrooooooooooong!" sang Sugar happily.

And then I saw it! A huge factory, poking up out of the sea.

"And that, of course..." said Tinselpants, pausing for effect, "...is AFRICA!"

Hannah giggled.

Below us a hairy white beast was waving Blaze down to land.

"And that white thing" continued Tinselpants pointing. "is a fat – and incredibly rare – snow zebra. You don't often see them standing on their back legs like that!"

Blaze landed with a bump next to the thing that was definitely not a snow zebra. It was

more like a shaggy white rug with a face.

"A yeti!" gasped Hannah.

"Welcome to...chocolates mines!" said the yeti smiling.

His voice made me think of a cave-man with a bit of grizzly bear thrown in but...

"Chocolate **mines**?" I hissed to Hannah. "Doesn't chocolate come from **beans**?"

Hannah shrugged.

"Just go with it," she suggested.

Two more yetis were heading over now. These ones had Christmassy ties clipped to their chests.

"Me Yanny!" said the biggest yeti, then he pointed to his friend saying, **"Him Dave! We run**

chocolate mines. You welcome!"

"Thank you soooooooooooooooooooo muuuuuuuuch," sang Sugar. "We're on our way to see Santa. He's a friend of mine."

The yetis looked impressed and Sugar smiled.

"So I was wondering if we could have a quick tour for the kids?" she winked. "Maybe a free sample or twooooo?"

The yetis nodded enthusiastically.

I'm guessing they didn't get many visitors out in the middle of the sea!

They hurried us into a noisy building full of rattling machines and criss-crossing conveyor belts.

"First we dig chocolate rocks from mines deep in ground under sea," explained Dave.

At that moment, an elevator door pinged open and out stomped several yetis pushing wheelbarrows full of huge brown rocks.

"Yetis bring choc-rocks here." added Yanny, pointing at the brown chunks.

We watched as the yetis took turns tipping out their wheelbarrows onto the nearest conveyor belt.

"We keep going!" cried Yanny, grabbing Blaze by the wing and pulling him along.

The next room was full of pipes as wide as water slides and copper-coloured funnels.

"Here - feed choc-rocks down pipes," Dave pointed. **"Down, down, down. Deep! Past lava in centre of earth. Lava melt chocolate."**

"Then - hot chocolate come back!" boomed Yanny, happily.

He walked over to a wide red pipe poking up through the floor. On its side was an old fashioned brass tap and when he twisted it, hot chocolate gushed out into the sink below.

"TA-DA!" he said proudly.

Yanny filled several mugs, handing one to each of us. It was not especially hot, but it tasted delicious.

"How long does this all take?" asked Hannah, sipping her almost-warm chocolate.

Yanny beamed and held up 3 claws.

"Only 3 years!" he said proudly.

He tossed a chunk of choc-rock high into the air and then caught it in an empty mug with a clunk.

A few nearby yetis applauded and he bowed as if he'd performed a cool circus trick.

I think Yanny was a bit of a show-off!

I looked at Blaze and I could tell he was thinking the same thing.

"Erm, can I....?" asked Blaze, taking the mug.

He shot a tiny blast of flames at the mug and at once the choc-rock began to bubble and froth.

"Wooooah!" said Dave, clearly impressed but

"NO!" snapped Yanny. **"Have good way to**

heat chocolate already!"

Yanny snatched back his mug and stomped away muttering something about "traditions" but Dave was grinning at Blaze.

"You stay!" he boomed happily. **"We talk new ways heat chocolate! We have... HOT CHOCOLATE REVOLUTION!"**

Tinselpants nodded enthusiastically.

"A revolution," he explained turning to us, "is a sort of snow zebra party where everyone spins around as fast as they can! Like this!"

Tinselpants began spinning to demonstrate.

"Whooopeeeeeeee," he cried going faster and faster. "Revoluuuuuuution!"

Meanwhile, Dave was still grinning at Blaze, waiting for an answer!

"Errrrm...well...ermmmm... I..." tried Blaze, looking desperately at Sugar for help.

"Gotta go!" she sang, before adding with a cheeky wink, "Try Googling something called a microwave."

"Googling?" asked Dave, puzzled, but Sugar was already ushering us out, back into the icy night.

CHAPTER EIGHT

On and on we flew, until at last the sea below became the frozen moonlit lands of the Arctic.

Now I've seen the Arctic on TV and maybe you have too. It always looks empty, right?

Well, the real Arctic wasn't like that at all because bounding all over the ice were cats. And I mean BIG CATS!

There were lions and tigers and cheetahs...or they might have been leopards (I get those two muddled).

But anyway, the important thing was that

they were **all grey and white!** In fact every single one looked like a black and white photo of itself.

"Amazing!" whispered Hannah.

"Indeed!" agreed Tinselpants. "Those are Santa's elves and you'll notice..."

"They're endangered cats," interrupted Sugar. "Santa lets them hide up here, where they can be safe."

"But they're all grey!" I pointed out.

"Santa does that with his Christmas magic!" said Blaze. "It helps keep them hidden. Now hold on, I'm going to take us down!"

As we came in to land, I noticed that the cats were not just running about wildly. They were actually playing a game, trying to knock three huge balls towards a candy cane arch!

"Oh goody!" sang Sugar, "I love a bit of Pawball."

"What's Pawball?" asked Hannah.

"It's a bit like that football thing you told me about!" explained Blaze. "Except it's got three balls and only one goal."

"And it's a thousand times betteeeeer!" sang Sugar.

"Sugar is a BIG Pawball fan," explained Blaze looking between Sugar and the game with a worried expression. "She really, er... gets into it."

He was right about that! Sugar was already singing advice.

"No, no, nooooooo," she cried. **"What is this? Pawball for Kitteeeeens?!"**

Blaze's blue cheeks flushed purple with embarrassment.

"Sugar!" he hissed, but she wasn't listening.

"Come ooooooooon!" yelled Sugar. **"My granny's pet hamster could have knocked that further... with its legs tied behind it back!"**

"Let's get going!" pleaded Blaze but just then a grumpy looking lion blew a whistle.

"Penaltyyyyyyyyy!" screamed Sugar.

The lion scowled across at her but it looked like she was right.

One of the balls was placed down on the ice and a grey and white tiger prowled towards it, eyeing the candy cane goal.

Then, from nowhere... Sugar flew onto the pitch and **took the penalty herself**, magically belting the massive ball through the candy cane arch!

"GOOOOOOOOAL!"

she sang, sliding to her knees on the ice.

"YES! YES! YES!"

"Oh no, no, no" whimpered Blaze beside me.

He was right to be worried! Every single cat was glaring at Sugar, looking **murderous!**

"What a goal. I. . ." Sugar stopped suddenly as she **finally** noticed the furious cats heading her way.

"**Oh...erm**," spluttered Sugar. "**I...**"

But at that moment, the big cats froze.

Hannah had seen it too. She made a squeaky noise and pointed into the distance with a shaky hand.

Coming towards us across the ice were several huge polar bears...

...looking extremely scary and horribly ready to eat us!

CHAPTER NINE

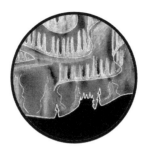

It turns out that polar bears in real life are a lot bigger than they look on TV.

But before we had much time to worry about that they paced straight past us.

Towards the pawball team!

I wasn't sure which animal would win in a fight between a bear and a tiger, but it looked like we were about to find out!

The polar bears reached the middle of the pitch and paused just inches from the cats.

No one moved.

No one even breathed.

I could hear my own heart hammering in my chest and I had a weird urge to yell just to stop everything being so tense.

But then...

...one of the polar bears grinned ...

...and then he did an extremely long and incredibly noisy...FART!

PPPPPPPPPHHHHHHHHHHHHH

AAAAAAAAAAAAAAAAAAAAAA

AAAAART – AAA – AAAA-

PAAAARPAPAPP

PAAAARB!

PAAAP!

It just went on and on. **And that wasn't all!**

A magnificent cloud of purple gas was puffing out of his bum and rising into the sky.

And then, all at once, the other polar bears started to join in, adding their own purple clouds.

PAAAAAAA AAAAARP!

Suddenly, everyone was at it!

The big cats trumped, adding swirls of pink.

PARP!

Seals popped up onto the ice and trumped enormous clouds of neon green, before splashing away.

PARP!

Snowmen appeared from nowhere, shooting into the air on clouds of blue and Tinselpants bounced off to join them!

The colours swirled together, drifting out to fill the sky.

"Wait..." I gasped, "is that...?"

"Yep," agreed Blaze nodding. "The Northern Lights!"

"More like the northern trumps," giggled Sugar.

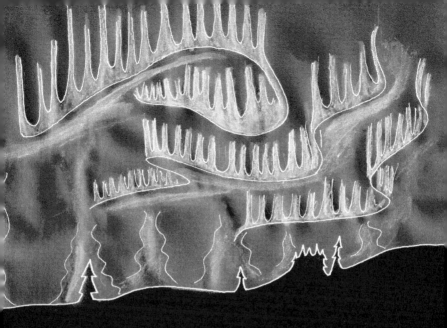

The sky blazed with impossible colours and it was breathtaking...in more ways than one, if you know what I mean!

I'm not sure how long we stood there, holding our noses and watching the neon trumps swirling together...

...but eventually a loud clapping brought us all back to our senses.

"BRAVO! BRAVO!" bellowed a jolly voice. **"Excellent show. Really, really well done!"**

Hannah gasped.

An old but sprightly man was clapping enthusiastically and congratulating each farter in turn as he made his way through the crowd.

"Is that...?" whispered Hannah.

"Yep!" nodded Blaze with a grin. "That's Santa!"

CHAPTER TEN

It really was him!

Santa was walking across the ice towards us, shaking hands and slapping shoulders. I'm guessing he didn't always come to watch the show because the crowds were crazy excited!

"Did you see that!" squealed a seal to anyone who would listen.

"He high-fived me...

And with that, the seal flopped back

I'm never washing this hand again.

into the sea, trying to swim with one flipper out of the water. Santa was wearing a bright blue coat and a silver bobble hat. His rather large bottom was squeezed into a pair of silver snowflake leggings and on his feet were silver snow boots.

"Are you sure that's him?" asked Hannah, looking puzzled. *"Doesn't Santa wear red?"* Trust Hannah to be thinking about fashion at a time like this! **"Red is for Christmas Eve,"** sang Sugar. **"Blue is for..."**

But we never found out what blue was for because at that moment Santa spotted us.

"What's this? What's this?" he bellowed. **"You're not arctic folk! Have you come to join my Elf Training**

program?"

"**Yes! Yes! YES!**" squeaked Sugar, turning a yellowy gold colour with excitement.

"No!" said Blaze firmly and Sugar glared at him.

"**Well, which is it?**" Santa chuckled, looking between them.

"Excuse me, Santa," said Hannah, stepping forward. "We're actually here because we need your help."

Santa turned to his attention to Hannah at once.

"**My help?**" he said. "**But why?**"

As Hannah and I took turns to explain Santa's eyes grew wide.

"**Good gracious!**" he cried. "**What a naughty elf! You were right to come for a magical gift! Now, let me see...**"

He turned and pulled a large sack from just behind him.

Now you don't have to believe me but I promise - that sack just appeared from nowhere!

He rummaged around in the velvety red bag then smiled up at Hannah.

"So, what is it that you really want?" he asked, his eyes twinkling.

"I want it to go back to how it was" said Hannah, sounding determined, "when the elf was just a toy and we still had Grandad's sleigh."

"Ahhhhhh," Santa nodded. **"That is called restoration. Very tricky business. And rarely a gift. It often takes a lot of work!"**

"Getting an elf was my idea so I'll do whatever work it takes to fix things," said Hannah, standing a bit taller. "I'm just asking for a bit of magical help."

Santa beamed his approval.

"Very well then," he said.

He thrust his arm deeper into
the sack and pulled out...

...a bit of **wooden plank.**

Hannah took it, trying to
hide her obvious disappointment.

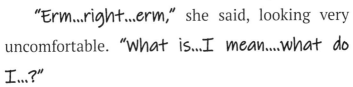

"Erm...right...erm," she said, looking very
uncomfortable. "What is...I mean....what do
I...?"

**"I'm sure you'll know what to
do..."** he said, giving Tinselpants a meaningful
look, "...**when the time is right!"**

Tinselpants checked over his shoulder to see
if Santa was perhaps looking at someone else.

When there was no one there, he looked a bit
alarmed.

Hannah didn't look very thrilled either. I
could see her point. If Santa's plan depended on
Tinselpants knowing something useful, then we
were in BIG trouble.

"And what about you?" asked Santa, turning in my direction. **"What would you like?"**

"Me?" I asked and he nodded.

I thought hard. A gift from Santa. Anything. This was a big opportunity.

"Well," I began, trying to buy myself some time, "since I went to bed, I've

 ridden a dragon across the sea

met the chocolate mine yetis

 watched my first game of paw-ball

and seen the Northern Lights be farted across the sky.

That's a lot of good stuff for one night!"

"Indeed?" nodded Santa.

"I honestly can't think what could make this night better!" I shrugged, grinning.

Santa chuckled, looking delighted.

"Then I see you already possess the greatest gift of all."

"Excuse me Santa Claus Sir, she doesn't," worried Blaze, "You haven't given..."

"Contentment!" interrupted Santa, giving Blaze a stern glare. **"That is the greatest gift! Those who find the good in each day or, in this case, each night... need nothing more."**

I nodded. Unlike Hannah with her wooden plank gift, I think I actually understood.

I was pretty lucky!

"I'd like a new dress, Santa. If you're asking," sang Sugar.

"Actually, my dear, I was only asking the children," sighed Father

Christmas.

"**Of course, of course!**" sang Sugar with a wink. "**Happy to wait until Christmas morning. No big deal!**"

She faked a cough.

"**Silver...cough-cough...with matching shoes!**" coughed Sugar, giving him another cheeky wink.

He ignored her, squinting at the sky.

"**Not long until morning,**" he said. "**Might you need a little help to get home?**"

"Yes please, Santa Claus Sir," nodded Blaze.

Santa grinned.

"**Well alright then! This calls for some magical wind!**"

Everyone stumbled back slightly, thinking of the farty Northern Lights.

"**Ho Ho Ho! Not that kind of wind,**" laughed Santa. "**I was thinking of**

The North Wind."

From somewhere very far away, I heard the sound of Christmas bells and a fierce breeze gusted against my cheeks.

Only Blaze seemed to realize what was happening.

"Climb on!" he yelled, as the wind whipped up around us. "Quickly everyone!"

We clambered onto his back just in in the nick of time. A blizzard of snowflakes had begun to whirl around us.

"HO HO HO!" bellowed Santa over the storm.

"MERRY CHRISTMAS!"

I looked around to wave goodbye but he had already disappeared.

Blaze rose up into the air and I squeezed my eyes shut against the snow as Sugar's voice rang out over the storm.

"The north wind doth blooooooooow. . ." she squealed.

Only Sugar could be louder than a blizzard!

I buried my face under my arms to keep warm. It was bitterly cold.

"...and we shall have snoooooooooooow. . ." sang Sugar.

Something was wrong. It felt like Blaze was flying downwards again. Had we forgotten something?

"...and what will poor Robin do theeeeeeeeen?" screeched Sugar.

"I think we are about to find out," yelled

Blaze.

"**What**?" sang Sugar.

"What the 'poor Robin' will do!" shouted Blaze. "Look! Here comes General Red!"

I opened my eyes.

We were already back home, zipping through the sky, just over our school. And General Red was soaring towards us.

"ABOUT TIME!" he shouted. **"DID YOU GET THE MAGICAL GIFT?"**

Hannah nodded and waved her plank.

"WELL, I'VE FOUND HIM," yelled the General, **"BUT YOU WON'T BELIEVE WHAT HE'S DONE! LOOK!"**

General Red pointed his wing and we peered down through the last of the snowflakes.

Oh no!

CHAPTER ELEVEN

In the deserted school car park was a mountain of beautifully decorated Christmas trees. And standing next to it...was Elfie!

"NOT INVITED TO THEIR STUPID TREE PARTY, EH?" he muttered. "WELL, WHEN I'M DONE, THERE'LL BE NO MORE PARTIES TO MISS!"

We had managed to land without being seen. Now we were crouched behind a tall hedge spying on the crazy elf and trying to make a plan.

"I HATE TREES," screamed Elfie, **"I HATE TREE PARTIES AND I HATE CHRISTMAS!"**

He wiggled his fingers and cackled wildly.

"YOU'RE NOTHING BUT A BUNCH OF OLD TWIGS!" he yelled, pointing at the pile of

trees, **"AND YOU'LL BURN LIKE A BUNCH OF OLD TWIGS!"**

In the moonlight, Elfie held a box to the sky and gave it a gleeful rattle.

MATCHES!

"Oh no!" groaned Blaze. "Where did he get those?"

"What do we do?" squeaked Hannah.

Elfie had started rummaging around in the trees.

"MAYBE THERE'S A FLOATY FAIRY DRESS IN HERE SOMEWHERE," he muttered.

"THAT WOULD GET A GOOD FIRE STARTED,"

Sugar's skin turned red with fury.

"**Where's that nutcracker when you need it**," she growled, but Tinselpants looked thoughtful.

"Let's tie him up with Tinsel," he whispered. "Tinsel is full of Christmas magic! It would be unbreakable!"

"Are you sure?" asked Hannah.

"Look, I know I haven't been a great guide..." he began.

"**You've been a terrible guide**," agreed

Sugar grinning.

"**well that's fair,**" he admitted. "**You see, the truth is, I don't know anything about the world...**"

"**You don't say!**" muttered Sugar.

"**I just really wanted to see it...**" Tinselpants continued a little sadly, "**...just once.**"

Hannah patted his shoulder, kindly.

"**well now you have!**" she smiled.

"**Yes. I have!**" he agreed, looking brighter. "**And I might not know much, but I do know about Christmas!**" he added firmly. "**You can trust me about the tinsel.**"

I looked at Hannah and she shrugged.

"OK! Let's do it!" I decided. "Once Elfie is tied up we can work out what we do with the gift."

"**But it's just a chunk of wood,**" wailed

Hannah.

Now it was Sugar's turn to pat her arm.

"You stay here with Tinselpants and try to work it out," she suggested. **"We'll go get some tinsel."**

It wasn't a perfect plan but it was the best we could do.

So while Hannah and Tinselpants prodded at the plank, the rest of us darted around to the other side of the tree mountain and started to untangle the first strand of tinsel.

It was going quite well until...

CLINK...Clink...clink...

Somehow a single bauble had bounced to the ground.

"WHO'S THERE?" snapped the Elf.

And my stomach flipped as a familiar voice answered,

"ME!"

Peering past trees I saw **Hannah** stepping

out in to the car park. What was she doing?

"YOU!" snarled Elfie. "COME TO STOP ME, HAVE YOU?"

"Yes!" admitted Hannah looking calm and brave. "Yes, I thought I might try."

Seriously, WHAT was she doing? This wasn't in the plan!

"AND WHERE'S THE REST OF YOUR SILLY LITTLE GANG?" sneered Elfie, glancing round.

I looked at Sugar and Blaze. We had only unraveled one string of tinsel but we were out of time. I jumped onto Blaze's back and Sugar nodded.

"We're right here!" I yelled and together we swooped out of our hiding place.

We dived towards him madly. Then round and round we went, tangling him as best we could with the single sparkling strand.

Elfie snarled and struggled to break free but for once Tinselpants had been right!

The tinsel was unbreakable!

"WHAT IS THIS?!?!!" screeched Elfie, as he realised he was stuck. **"SLEIGH! HELP ME!"**

The sleigh immediately shot out its magical force field, just as it had back in our garden. But this time Elfie was too far away.

"NO GOOD, SLEIGH!" cried the elf. **"TRY SOMETHING ELSE! QUICKLY!"**

Instantly, the sleigh began shooting candy

canes like arrows in every direction!

TWANG, THUNK, WHIZZ, THUNK!

Blaze swung left and right trying to dodge, but Sugar had other ideas.

She swooped down, snatching up a candy cane arrow as she went and began to beat up the sleigh with it's own Christmassy weapon.

"Stop it, you naughty sleigh! Stop - it - right - now!"

Elfie was staggering around in the tinsel but somehow he'd managed to wriggle an arm free. He yanked a string of fairy lights from a nearby tree and with an evil laugh he threw the lights like a lasso... straight at me and Blaze!

Blaze tried to swerve but his wing got tangled and everyone knows fairy lights are impossible to untangle!

Down on the ground, Elfie was holding tight to the other end of the lights.

We had just become the world's most Christmassy dragon kite!

With a crazed laugh Elfie started to tug us towards him.

"Let go of the lights!" yelled Hannah.

"We can't!" I screamed. "We're tangled!"

Blaze flapped his wings furiously, but it was no use. Elfie was pulling us closer and closer!

"The gift, Hannah," I screamed. "Use the

gift!"

Hannah looked down at the plank of wood in her hands.

"But I don't..." she began.

"Well, I DO!" yelled Tinselpants, rushing out from behind the hedge to stand by Hannah's side.

"Hey elf!" he cried, "I'm putting you back on the shelf, where you belong!"

Elfie twitched.

"WHAT... WHAT SHELF?" he sneered, but he glanced around nervously. "YOU DON'T HAVE A SHELF!"

"Oh yes, I do!" yelled Tinselpants.

"meeeeeeeeeeeeerRY CHRISTMAS!"

And with that Tinselpants snatched the plank from Hannah and bounced towards Elfie, leaping over Christmas trees like a snowman ninja.

Elfie's eyes grew wide. He turned to run but he was too late. Tinselpants swung the plank through the air and hit him on the bum with a mighty

"NO!" he cried. "NO! NO! NO!"

With an explosion of magical dust the chunk of wood stuck fast to Elfie's bottom. He clawed and yanked at it, but it was no use. It wouldn't budge!

Because as you've probably guessed, it wasn't just any old plank...

Santa had given Hannah... a magical Shelf!

"NO!" screamed Elfie. "NOOOOOOOOOO!"

He was shrinking back to toy size now. He tried desperately to light a match but his hands fumbled. They were turning back into mittens.

"**YOU BRATS!**" he screeched, staggering towards us, "**I'M GOING TO...**"

But before he could finish his face froze. His tiny body went limp and he flopped to the floor ... and lay still.

On the other side of the car park, the sleigh stopped fighting but Sugar didn't seem to notice.

She just kept on whacking it.

Maybe she thought she was winning!

I slid down from Blaze's back as Hannah came to join us. It felt like the right moment for someone to say something wise.

"Erm...All's well that ends well," I suggested.

"Yep," agreed Hannah. "I guess so. Although we should probably go get Grandad's sleigh before Sugar smashes it to bits!"

CHAPTER TWELVE

I cradled Grandad's sleigh decoration close to my chest. It looked fragile again, now it was back to the normal size.

Hard to believe it had been belting us with candy canes just a few moments ago.

"**We did it!**" sang Sugar who was now eating her candy cane.

"And we couldn't have done it without you, Tinselpants!" said Hannah.

"Thanks," he blushed. "Meeeerry

Christmas!"

"Now what do we do about all these trees," I wondered aloud. "We don't know where they came from but we can't just leave them here…"

"Imagine people waking up and finding their tree gone!" cried Hannah. It's absolutely awful!"

"**Don't worry**," smiled Sugar. **"It's fixable. We just need a little magical sooooooooong."**

Blaze pulled a face, but before he could complain Sugar started to sing.

We've been through such a lot! Our elf-he totally lost the plot, yeah-eh-ah-eh yeeeeeeeeah!

"Could you please get to the point, Sugar," interrupted Blaze with a shiver. "The children are getting cold."

Sugar scowled.

"Fine," she muttered grumpily.

"Christmas trees
Full of light
Turn to rockets
Blazing bright!"

She took a theatrical bow.

"Short and sweet," she announced. **"Just like me!"**

The pile of trees began to rustle.

"10, 9, 8, 7..." sang Sugar.

The rustle became a wobble and on the trees ornaments began to clink and clank together.

"6, 5, 4, 3," shouted Sugar.

Suddenly, the bottom of each

ROAR OF NOISE!

"Sugar, what have you done?!" screamed Hannah but Sugar just kept counting down.

"2,1, BLAST OFF!" she screamed.

With a **MASSIVE EXPLOSION** the first Christmas tree shot into the sky like a bristly green rocket. The rest of the trees followed, exploding fire and zooming back to their homes.

In no time at all, not a single bauble was left. The school car park was completely empty.

"Amazing!" smiled Hannah, watching the last tree whiz out of sight.

"Yes, yes. Very impressive," grumbled Blaze. "But now it's time for bed!"

He crouched down so we could climb onto his back. But just then, there was a snort as a golden triceratops plodded out of a nearby bush.

"Glitzen!" cried Hannah. "You're safe!"

The dinosaur looked blankly at her for a second then returned to munching the frosty grass.

Sugar flew to Glitzen's side and gave him a friendly stroke, her face full of mischief.

"**How about a little race**?" she called to Blaze wiggling her eyebrows.

"It's far too late for silliness like that," said Blaze crossly.

"I'm with the fairy!" cried Tinselpants and giggling the two of them climbed onto

Glitzen's back.

"Last one home's a big bummed bauble!" sang Sugar.

"Now, seriously…" tried Blaze but as always, Sugar wasn't listening.

"Giddyup!" she cried and Glitzen shot into the sky, leaving a trail of shimmering gold.

"Catch them, Blaze!" screamed Hannah.

"Pleeeeeeeeeease!"

"I'm wiiiinniiiiiiiiiiiiiiiiiiiiiiiiiiing!" called Sugar in her most annoying voice.

That seemed to decide things for Blaze.

He snorted flames and sprang into the sky after them...

...and we raced through the starry night, all the way home.

CHAPTER THIRTEEN

When I woke up under the Christmas tree the next morning, everything was strangely still and quiet.

Sugar and Blaze were lying lifeless on our pillows just like ordinary toys. And the tree looked completely normal, each ornament in its place.

Only one thing was different.

Outside, the whole world had been turned white with snow. And lots of it too.

"Hannah, wake up! Look!" I called.

Hannah rubbed her eyes and then stumbled over to join me at the window.

"Brilliant!" she smiled. "Let's get out there!"

But at that moment a strange red and green van pulled up in front of the house. And two even stranger men got out!

They were both wearing long green coats, white and green tights and bright red shoes.

"They look like Elfie!" whispered Hannah. "What's happening now?"

"Let's find out," I frowned.

The doorbell rang and we ran into the kitchen just as Dad opened the door.

"Sorry to disturb you, Sir, we got your address from the school" said one of the men, "I'm afraid we need to take the elf you won at the fair. There's been a product recall."

"Really?" said Dad, puzzled. "Why? What's wrong with it?"

"Ermmm...I think the, er, stitching is faulty," said one of the men, clearly making stuff up.

"It could lose its head," added the other man helpfully.

"Lose its head? More like, completely lose its mind!" whispered Hannah and we grinned.

"Oh, I see," said Dad looking like he didn't see at all. "Well, erm, here he is!"

We had left Elfie in the kitchen when we got home last night (guarded by General Red, of course, just in case) and now Dad held out the limp elf to one of the men.

As the man leaned forward his coat slipped open to reveal a green shirt with the words "Elf Squad" in gold lettering.

Hannah gasped. She'd seen it too.

"So, where's the replacement?" asked Dad brightly.

"Oh, don't worry, Sir," said the first man. "There isn't one,"

"Your house is now completely Elf free," agreed the second man. "Would you like us to take that yucky old robin too?"

He was looking at General Red with an odd expression. Could he sense the magic still lingering around the old toilet roll?

"Certainly not!" cried Dad. **"That's a family heirloom, that is!"**

"Up to you, Sir," shrugged the man and with a nod to his companion they

both walked away down the path.

Dad closed the door and then, realizing we were there, he began to look uncomfortable.

"Erm... Bit of bad news..." he started.

"We heard," I interrupted. "The elf's gone."

I tried my best not to grin with relief.

"I'm so sorry," said Dad. "We could always get another one from..."

"NO!"

Hannah and I had almost shouted it.

Dad looked at us curiously.

"Dad," said Hannah quickly changing the subject, "Do you think people can trump different colours?"

Dad's face brightened immediately.

"Excellent question!" he cried. "Fetch me all the jelly beans we have! We will conduct an experiment."

"No way," said Mum coming in. "That sounds like a way to find out if people can be **sick** in different colours."

"But this is important science!" exclaimed Dad, pretending to be offended.

Mum laughed.

"On second thoughts, maybe you'd need to colour them after they leak out," said Dad, tapping his chin. "Hannah start eating as many normal beans as you can! **I'll go fetch some crayons...and we'll need some kind of net!"**

"Or..." said Mum firmly, "We could all go and play in the snow."

The snow! I'd almost forgotten all that brilliant snow!

Dad nodded.

"Yes!" he agreed cheerfully. "Let's go build a snowman and see if **they** fart in a colour."

"Oh, we already know the answer to that," said Hannah giving me a secret wink. "Snowman farts are blue!"

And with that, we rushed out into the snow to play.

Quiz: Which character are you?

1. You are eating Christmas dinner when someone notices that there are no sprouts. Do you:

a) Order everyone to stop eating and search for the missing vegetables at once.

b) Throw your plate at the wall and shout, "Who cares? I love mess!"

c) Explain that sprouts are actually aliens' bogies, first bought back from space in 1982.

2. You are watching the school nativity play when the music stops working. Do you:

a) Attack one of the wise men, screaming, "This is not a real king! Impostor! trickery!"

b) Pull out all the cables pretending to help, but then use the wires to tie up all the teachers.

c) Explain that the sudden quiet is to help relax the trump-wuzzles before their traditional dance.

3. You are given a chocolate advent calendar. Do

you:

a) Shout, "Who imprisoned these poor defenceless chocolates?" and peck every window to free them.

b) Crawl into the calendar and tape all the windows shut from the inside, trapping yourself.

c) Wear it as a hat.

4. You notice some mistletoe hanging over the kitchen door. Do you:

a) Eat it... then demand everyone searches for it because it's gone missing.

b) Tie it to people's toes while they sleep, so when they wake up they have to kiss their own feet.

c) Explain that what people think are mistletoe berries are actually blobs of frozen Janglebum poo, and are delicious with ice cream.

If answered mostly A, you're General Red. Mostly B, you're Elfie. Mostly C, you're Tinselpants. Meeeeeeerry Christmas!

Who would you draw farting the Northern Lights?

What did the snowman's hat say to the scarf?
You hang around while I go on ahead!

M	E	O	P	P	B	S	S	A	P	T	S	L	W
A	G	L	I	T	Z	E	N	R	E	G	N	E	P
L	S	L	B	H	G	I	E	L	S	B	N	M	I
B	R	T	A	L	L	I	E	L	F	I	E	C	S
S	T	N	A	P	L	E	S	N	I	T	H	U	A
A	A	H	T	B	B	B	S	U	Y	R	H	T	O
A	R	S	T	I	N	L	T	C	I	E	R	G	A
T	Y	L	R	L	S	I	G	S	N	F	T	A	E
N	E	G	T	A	I	U	T	I	O	O	N	I	R
A	B	L	A	T	L	M	B	R	A	W	N	A	L
S	L	T	S	L	A	O	I	L	Y	N	G	C	L
R	A	G	R	S	R	S	P	U	T	U	N	F	I
M	Z	P	H	L	S	E	B	S	S	A	E	L	A
N	E	P	A	W	B	A	L	L	M	S	T	I	I

ROBIN	**SLEIGH**
GLITZEN	**SUGAR**
POLAR	**ELFIE**
BLAZE	**CHRISTMAS**
TINSELPANTS	**YETI**
PAWBALL	**SANTA**

Go to www.jennyyork.com for lots more FUN!

Look out for:

Printed in Great Britain
by Amazon